What If...

Story by Regina J. Williams ✳ **Illustrations by Doug Keith**

ILLUMINATION Arts

PUBLISHING, L.L.C.

I know it's
time for bed, Mom,
but what if…

My teddy bear could fly,
so I could ride him
to the nearest rainbow
and then stay awhile
to play.

And what if…

Dogs really did grow on
dogwood trees,
and I could pick a puppy
from a branch
and name her
Millie.

And what if . . .

Butterflies could sing,
and one flew in my window
every night to sing me
a lullaby.

And what if …

I had my own
special garden where I planted
candy hearts, marshmallow eggs,
and chocolate Santas, all in a row.

And what if...

Clouds suddenly became the
creatures they look like
and put on a show in the sky
just for me and my friends.

And what if . . .

Flowers tasted like lollipops,
and they grew really big
all around my bed.

And what if . . .

People everywhere would dance
and sing and be happy.

And there was only sunshine and love,
so all the scary monsters
would go away forever.

And what if . . .

All the trees would suddenly shrink
until they were the size of flowers,
and I could pick a bouquet
just for you, Mom.

And what if . . .

A shooting star
would fly into my pocket
and bring magic to my heart
forever.

And what if...

It snowed silver and gold snowflakes
that sparkled like diamonds
and tasted like
peppermint ice cream.

And what if . . .

I made a great big seahorse out of clay,
then it came alive
and splashed around with me
in the bathtub.

And what if . . .

I had a real kangaroo for a pet,
and I could sleep in her pouch,
and her name was
Cornflower.

And what if...

I could raise my arms to touch the sky
and make a special rain
that would clean
the whole world.

And, Mom, what if . . . what if . . .

I had wings
and could fly through the
clouds, and ... and ...

"And now my little angel,
what if . . . we turn off the light,
so you can turn on your dream light
and dream your sweet dreams
all night long."

PUBLISHING, L.L.C.
P.O. Box 1865, Bellevue, WA 98009
Tel: 425-968-5097 ★ Fax: 425-968-5634
liteinfo@illumin.com ★ www.illumin.com

Publisher's Appreciation:
We greatly appreciate the diligent and creative assistance of Mie Morikubo in formatting this new softcover version of our timeless children's classic.

Library of Congress Cataloging-in-Publication Data
Williams, Regina, 1958-
    What if- / written by Regina J. Williams; illustrated by Doug Keith.
      p. cm.
    Summary: A child speculates about flying teddy bears, flowers that taste like candy, gold snowflakes, and more.
    ISBN 0-935699-22-8; 978-0-935699-22-7; 978-0-9855417-3-6
     [1. Bedtime-Fiction. 2. Imagination-Fiction. 3. Dreams-Fiction.] I. Keith, Doug, ill. II. Title.

PZ7.W6678 Wh 2001
[E]-dc21
                                                                                               00-054065

INSPIRE EVERY CHILD FOUNDATION

A portion of the profits from this book will be donated to Inspire Every Child, a non-profit foundation dedicated to helping disadvantaged children around the world. This organization provides inspirational children's books to individuals and groups that are directly involved in supporting the welfare of children. Your help in supporting this crucial cause would be greatly appreciated. For more information, please visit www.inspire-every-child.org.

Third Printing 2013
Published in the United States of America
Printed by Shanghai Chenxi Printing Co., Ltd.
Book Designer: Molly Murrah, Murrah & Company, Kirkland, WA

Author, Regina Williams

What If… began as a game between Regina Williams and her daughter Kayla. "One of us would say 'What if … could happen?' Then the other one would try to create an even more imaginative idea. The energy would build," Regina says, "as we came up with wild and fun possibilities, many of which are included in my story."

Growing up on a farm in northeast Texas, much of Regina's childhood entertainment came from books. A Magna Cum Laude graduate from the University of Texas, she is a speech and language pathologist in public schools. Regina and her husband live in the small town of New Boston, Texas with their daughters, Kayla and Grace. They also share their home with Millie, a miniature dachshund who is pleased to be featured in the story. What If… is Regina's first book.

Illustrator, Doug Keith

Doug Keith was delighted to illustrate What If… because of its focus on imagination. "This book provides an excellent opportunity to let your imagination soar and spiral way out of control!"

Doug modeled the main character after his daughter, Corie Lyn, who wasn't exactly thrilled to be portrayed as a boy. Corie Lyn's favorite teddy bear, Abner, and the family cat Merlin, also had modeling duties.

After remodeling his Seattle home to create a spacious studio, Doug now commutes to work in comfy slippers. Widely known for his alphabet posters, he has illustrated three other award-winning books for Illumination Arts, Something Special, The Errant Knight, and The Whoosh of Gadoosh.

Doug received his professional training at the Newark School of Fine and Industrial Arts. A versatile artist, he had received numerous accolades, including an Emmy for television graphics. His playful illustrations in What If… are a combination of watercolor and colored pencil.

More inspiring picture books from Illumination Arts

Just Imagine
John M. Thompson and George Schultz/Wodin, ISBN 978-0-9740190-6-2
Ready for fun and adventure? Who knows what might happen as we set our minds free and our imaginations take flight! Anything is possible when we *Just Imagine*.

Something Special
Terri Cohlene/Doug Keith, ISBN 978-0-9740190-1-7
A curious little frog finds a mysterious gift outside his home near the castle moat. It's *Something Special*… What can it be?

Am I a Color Too?
Heidi Cole/Nancy Vogl/Gerald Purnell, ISBN 978-0-9740190-5-5
A young interracial boy wonders why people are labeled by the color of their skin. Seeing that people dream, feel, sing, dance, and love regardless of their color, he asks, *Am I a Color, Too?*

Mrs. Murphy's Marvelous Mansion
Emma Roberts/Robert Rogalski, ISBN 978-0-9740190-4-8
Mrs. Murphy's snobbish neighbors are convinced that her strange little house should be torn down – until she invites them to come for lunch. As they wander through *Mrs. Murphy's Marvelous Mansion,* the neighbors have a surprising change of heart, learning that beauty on the inside matters more than beauty on the outside.

Little Yellow Pear Tomatoes
Demian Elainé Yumei/Nicole Tamarin, ISBN 978-0-9740190-2-4
In this enchanting story, we ponder the never-ending circle of life through the eyes of a young girl, who marvels at all the energy and collaboration it takes to grow *Little Yellow Pear Tomatoes*.

We Share One World
Jane E. Hoffelt/Marty Husted, ISBN 978-0-9701907-8-9
Wherever we live – whether we work in the fields, the waterways, the mountains or the cities – all people and creatures share one world.

A Mother's Promise
Lisa Humphrey/David Danioth, ISBN 978-0-9701907-9-6
A lifetime of sharing begins with the sacred vow a woman makes to her unborn child.

Your Father Forever
Travis Griffith/Raquel Abreu, ISBN 978-0-9740190-3-1
A devoted father promises to guide, protect, and respect his beloved children. Transcending the boundaries of culture and time, this is the perfect expression of a parent's never-ending love.

To view our whole collection, please visit us at **www.illumin.com.**